And ANOTHER SMILE

A science fiction novelette by

SABER BAGHERY

Translated from Persian by

ALIREZA MAHDIPOUR

Order this book online at www.trafford.com
or email orders@trafford.com

Most Trafford titles are also available at major online book retailers.

Note for Librarians: A cataloguing record for this book is available from Library
and Archives Canada at www.collectionscanada.ca/amicus/index-e.html

Printed in Victoria, BC, Canada.

ISBN: 978-1-4269-1592-5 (sc)

Library of Congress Control Number: 2009934196

*Our mission is to efficiently provide the world's finest, most comprehensive book
publishing service, enabling every author to experience success. To find out how to
publish your book, your way, and have it available worldwide, visit us online at
www.trafford.com*

Trafford rev. 9/22/2009

 www.trafford.com

North America & international
toll-free: 1 888 232 4444 (USA & Canada)
phone: 250 383 6864 ♦ fax: 812 355 4082

Author: SABER BAGHERY

And ANOTHER SMILE

For the late Arthur Charles Clarke

And ANOTHER SMILE

Synopsis:

Carla Fritz, a German doctor specialized in zoo-biology and **biotronic** -which is a branch of genetic engineering science that focuses on the use of microchips and electronic equipments on unicellular- , and an English chief engineer by the name **Steve Blake** are on mission organized by The Strategic Research Organization of United Europe (**S.R.O.U.E**) to grow intellectual (DNA) s in the form of unicellular in some apt tropical climate conditions, and to make them yield to initial nervous stimuli. To achieve this goal, at first they are trained to live alone in adverse cut off conditions for eight weeks, and then they are sent to a remote region in the central African Sahara, a protected area of **Batangato**, far from civilization, by an automatic pilot system aircraft. Their mission is to terminate in twenty weeks' time.

The purpose of planning the mission in this way is, in general, to train efficient human resources for the organization, for the future conquests of far away worlds of the solar system. There is a close competence among the scientists of the European Community and their colleagues from the developing countries who are contributing in this project, such as China, India, Malaysia, and Iran. A colleague of Steve Blake, chief engineer **Saeed Saalvar** from Iran, who has a seven space voyages in his record, is also involved in this project.

Carla Fritz, proud of her pompous pedigree and ambitious, holds herself superior than the best members of the organization. She has some preoccupations beyond her job. With the aid of her brother **Michael Fritz**, another scientist of the organization, she has designed and made an apparatus called Radio **Telesthesia**, a device with the ability to transform various animals' behavioral patterns into basic factors of human behaviors. In order to test the efficiency of the device before obtaining a patent for her invention, she takes it with her, almost secretly, to the field of her mission. She has already done some extensive research which indicated the probability that she would encounter with disabilities of some African kings of the beasts (lions); a probability that will be realized, incidentally, by her own reckless exit from the provisional camp site. It has been for her occasional lapses of prudence that the password of the Research Satellite which is one of the tools of the mission is entrusted to Steve Blake, despite Carla's being the commander of this two-members-team mission. Steve Blake is notified to keep a close eye on both Carla and the missionary affairs.

Carla tries to underrate Steve's role in the mission by elaborate arguments and broils, but later she finds that this doesn't help, and that by some small efforts she can make Steve cooperate with her.

Steve saves Carla from the paws of a huge lion, inflicting a fatal injury to one of the lion's paws during the event. Carla seizes the opportunity, and by a preplanned scheme, performs a surgical operation on the wounded animal and transplants a very efficient artificial paw.

The beast is left at large, and his natural behavior in his new condition is monitored by satellite. The lion transforms into an arch-killer of the African Sahara, even attacking the animals that he didn't dare to confront before. He also kills all the rival males of his tribe. The sense of killing grows in him by and by. He fights with a crocodile deliberately, and his one natural paw is badly injured. This time the beast comes towards the lab site voluntarily, so that a second unparalleled artificial paw may be bestowed on him by human beings.

Carla and Steve can hardly believe what they see. They watch the events with much wonder and notice that by his shattering blows of his artificial paw the lion has destroyed the laser chargers which were serious barriers against any intruders, and has entered the lab site. They have to kill the fierce creature, despite Carla's boundless feeling for the feline, and this lion in particular.

Carla, who had been monitoring the behavior of this supposedly extinct lion of African Sahara by her Radio Telesthesia, adoring his behavioral factors such as fear, spite, anger, and so on, holds her apparatus in her hands to observe the lion's last behavioral factor just before Steve can finish him by shooting at him. She notices that the lion's full gallops turn into long leaps, as he charges at Steve. Carla manages to record the lion's behavioral pattern. She remembers that she had seen that pattern before, during her first encounter with the beast, when she was nearly dominated by him. That was, a smile, then ..., and another smile.

Chapter 1

There were just twenty minutes left for the end of the seven hours flight of Big Fort, a vertical flight aircraft, to a remote spot in Central African Sahara, the destination of the mission, and Dr Carla Fritz was growing tired of her efforts to sustain an elaborate smile on her face, as a demonstration of her self-confidence, to the expense of the English chief engineer Steve Blake; particularly as these two were the whole passengers on board.

During those seven hours Dr Fritz had skimmed all the favorite parts of magazines on the desk and electronic newspapers, and after a friendly yet unsuccessful conversation with Steve Blake which had ended up in the long-established Anglo-German conflict, and ultimately in that of their own, she then occupied herself with reviewing the processes of her present mission and spent her remaining time in her inward thoughts.

She wished for a rapid flight of this twenty minutes' time, so that she could get rid of engineer Blake as soon as she was settled down in her temporary camp and began to report to her boss. This was of course beyond her authority, yet easy for her by the help of Uncle Wilhelm, who didn't care for the so called preference of family relationship for rules. **Hans Wilhelm Fritz** was the head of the aristocratic noble Fritz family in German; a family that for generations enjoyed an influential decisive role in the courts of Reich Empire and the Kaisers, and by the time being the renowned family had increasingly developed their presence in the Strategic Research Organization of United Europe (S.R.O.U.E).

Hans Wilhelm Fritz, fifty three, was one of the five members of the managing board of the organization. His niece, Carla Fritz, twenty eight, holding PhDs in zoo-biology and biotronic, was a research scientist of the organization. Her brother Michael Fritz, thirty one, was a genius in planning laser systems and artificial intelligence for the organization, and their father **Olaf Fritz**, sixty, had once been another member of the managing board, who was replaced by his brother Wilhelm after his death in a dubious crash and explosion of two submarines three years before. And finally, there was **Thomas Fritz**, twenty three, son of the great Wilhelm and a ph. D student of nuclear physics, who had a bright prospect in the organization.

As the necessity of a B level research mission was proposed by the Biotronic Department to the managing board two months before, and was accepted after so much investigations and debates, the time for the mission was decided for twenty weeks, after a course of lonely life instructions for the candidates for eight weeks, and the Sahara Desert of the central Africa, the protected national park of Batangato was chosen as the locale of the mission. The number of the expeditionary forces was allotted as two, a chief engineer plus one of the eight prominent scientists of the Biotronic Department.

It was partly by luck and partly by the use of influence that young Carla Fritz was chosen from among the members of the topmost scientists. The chosen member from the engineering section was chief engineer Steve Blake, a specialist of specific constructions.

However, it was not easy for Carla to accept an Englishman as a colleague for twenty weeks long, though according to the slogan of the organization they had to cope and cooperate with each other as family members throughout their mission.

After the end of the lonely life training course, Carla went to see her Uncle Wilhelm, with some ideas in her mind. One of her great expectations was going to be realized by the mission. Beside the object of her mission, which was to cultivate intelligent unicellulars in some apt tropical climate conditions, she could do some personal research in her favorite area of interest. That is, she could study the life of large felines, and in fact the largest of them, the lions. Steve's presence was of course a serious problem for her researches, and she therefore wanted to get rid of him by means of her Uncle Wilhelm.

After going through the ceremonies of receiving congratulations by friends, acquaintances, and colleagues for her achievement in the course exam, she dragged Wilhelm to a less crowded corner of the party (which was made by her colleagues for the sake of her success) and said:

"Uncle, I hope you have had a glance for my records."

"Of course I did my dear." said Wilhelm, "You have got 89%, from the total ten basic diagrams."

"And what about this Mr. Blake?" asked Carla.

"Oh, Steve Blake, yes, he has got 86.2%, which means he is some degrees lower than you. He is an Englishman, of course."

"And what is the least permissible standard mark for the achievement?" pursued Carla.

"It is 84%," replied Wilhelm dubiously, detecting Carla's intention by her way of inquiring. "But I told you that he is an Englishman."

"This indicates that I am better than him, in site planning, setting reactors, preparation of field lab, direction finding, and even in winding the screws of the camp, which are wound in inverted direction, things which are mostly his specialty, but I learned them during 56 days from him and two others. And now, why must he accompany me for those same jobs, after all the trouble that I have taken for the lonely life training? Of course, he is a chief engineer, I admit, and can repair a wireless device in critical situations or turn a bike into a manual excavating drill, but I see no need for him in this expedition, as there are three spare back-ups for every tool in this trip. Moreover, he is chatty and he jokes a lot. I am afraid he won't let me finish my job in peace in twenty weeks' time..."

"You are pushing it too hard, my dear." interrupted Wilhelm, "I am just one member of the managing board, you know, and not the whole management. Moreover, there is no rule in the organization to let you have a B level research mission by yourself. If you insist, then wait for such a rule to be made. But, take it easy. You can contact me any time, in case of any problem in your career, or any probable bother of Steve Blake."

That was a considerable concession granted to Carla, she thought.

Carla started by a sound of the automatic pilot. After a short low whistle there was an announcement of the arrival:

"Ladies and gentlemen!" said a recorded voice, "Please be seated and fasten your seat-belts. We are going to land in three minutes, with a slight shake … Thank you for your cooperation."

Steve Blake, who had busied himself with his laptop, rushed to the automatic drink machine for his eighth cup of coffee. Time flied quickly. A sudden silence indicated that it was time for landing. The monitor on the wall inside the cabin offered vivid images of the surrounding area. The aircraft was just landing in the middle of a vast green meadow. There were a bunch of **Somor** and **Salam** trees a little afar, when Carla saw her most favorite sight that she might imagine. She watched with relish a herd of lions at rest, who started running away as the aircraft landed. Lionesses drove their little ones away by the push of their heads, and the younger lions followed them, all in flight. The leader of the herd, with his long abundant mane that covered his huge head except his face, looked backward severally, at the giant bird that had then perched on his dominion, and left.

The cabin door opened automatically and slowly, and the steps appeared before the passengers. Carla started to descend the steps before Steve, who was busy packing his pc, and Steve observed, with his typical joking mood, "After you!", when Carla was almost at the threshold. Carla lingered for a second, and then hurried down the steps. She was exasperated by Steve Blake, who wouldn't be shaken off.

She went to the provisional store which was then being lowered to the ground automatically. She stepped inside the store. She was walking towards the jeep, when her eye caught something, and stopped to scrutinize it. It was a black box, in a cylinder form, fixed high on the wall of the store near the entrance. It annoyed Carla, even more than Steve Blake himself, because it emitted infrasound waves that scared the lions more than the sound or sight of the aircraft. It was designed for the sole purpose of frightening the lions away, to provide a secure area for the field laboratory. It had been made by an Iranian chief engineer named Saeed Saalvar, as the first act of the developing countries' cooperation with the United European Strategic Research Organization. There was also another similar transmitting device that had to be fixed near the lab, high above a five meters post, to function from the time the field lab would be set up until the end of the mission. And that was Steve Blake's job.

Steve Blake was standing behind Carla at the time. He shuffled his shoes on the grass, to announce his presence. Carla got ahead of Steve, reaching for the jeep before him, and said, "I'll drive the car." Steve Blake shrugged indifferently, and took the seat beside the driver. The jeep of the research group came out of the belly of the aircraft and set out to survey the camp area. After they had explored the camp area thoroughly, Carla drove towards Somor and Salam trees and stopped by them.

"Let me clarify something first, Miss Dr fritz," said Steve Blake, assuming a rather serious tone. "From now on you and I shall have to be together for twenty weeks, whether willing or not. I don't know what the matter between you and me is, yet you are Carla and I am Steve, no matters friends or not. Because I can't imagine how to call you Dr Fritz at least fifty times a day."

Carla stared into Steve's eyes blankly, as if searching them for something. "Maybe we are not," she thought, "after I sent my report, of course." Then she had a better idea. She tried to look through Steve's character, to penetrate into his personality perhaps, hoping to persuade him in the future to cope with her in affairs which were beyond their missionary obligations. She got out of the car deliberately, and started towards the biggest tree, anticipating Steve's warning voice. She walked several paces but heard nothing. She walked a few steps farther, and was then almost twenty meters away from the car, still without any objection of Steve's. She turned round, with wonder and a little indignation, and looked behind.

"Have you forgotten anything?" said Steve, holding a 48 Wilson rifle in his hands and offering it to Carla. She was a bit disappointed by Steve's failure in quick warning, yet at the same time her hopes for his future cooperation grew. According to the restrict rules of the organization, in a field cruising they had not only to be together but also carry a 48 Wilson rifle, which was capable of killing a male elephant from a mile, together with a rocket launcher containing PN7 type anesthetizing capsules.

Anyone who wished to get out of the car was obliged to carry the Wilson rifle.

Carla turned back and got into the car.

Carla was regarded the leader of that two members team because the major goal of the mission was her task. She therefore gave up driving and sat on Steve's place. As Steve took his seat behind the steering wheel he said, in a half-serious tone, "Thank you, for your trust in me." And they came back to the camp.

They began unpacking things and setting up their private compartments at the bottom of the provisional store, inside the aircraft. Those special compartments were going to be their temporary camp for six days, during which they would be busy setting up the lab and build up the camp area. They would then move to the main camp and stay there until the end of their mission.

Steve served the first night dinner, after they had finished building up the temporary camp. After the meal they retired to their own lonely compartments. Steve had grown curiously taciturn, as if he had suspected Carla's intentions and had taken refuge in his solitude, to keep himself away from her probable designs.

Carla began setting up the satellite transmitter. She started the tiny motor to adjust the automatic antenna. As soon as the laser tracker set the antenna in its proper direction, she locked up the instrument. Then she sent the secret code of the operation, and the familiar sign of the organization (twelve circular stars) appeared on the monitor, and then the image of the central controlling operator.

Carla sent her report of the completion of stage one and two of the mission and then called Steve. Steve sent his reports, too, of the camp environment, and the transmission ended.

Steve worked with his laptop for a while and then went into his compartment, to go to bed. Carla retired to her room soon after him.

Chapter 2

"I will go, by one hour almost, when Steve is sound asleep." Carla decided, measuring her time. During that one hour she occupied herself with setting up her Radio Telesthesia, an instrument that was able to transform sounds, signs, and behaviors of various animals to one of the basic factors of human behavior. This device had been planned and manufactured by Carla, with considerable help of her brother Michael, but they had decided to test it secretly, in real conditions, before announcing the invention to the public and obtaining a patent for it and presenting it to the organization. Carla had therefore brought it to the field of her mission. There was also another secret thing among Carla's tools; a paw made of titanium, which was at least one of her two main reasons for taking part in that mission, if not her best one.

According to the statistics from African national parks, gathered by Carla before her expedition, and her diagram drawn out of the data, from fifty adult lions whose leadership probability were up to 80%, one was likely to be maimed by crucial injury. After that, he wouldn't survive longer than six or eight months, and was likely to die because of the harassments of the other lions of the group and downright neglect. 35% of this supposed disability would be imposed to the male leader of the group by men, and the remaining 65% by his strong rivals whose ambition for leadership had extremely grown. Even in that 65% too, men played an indirect role. That is, by threatening and invasion to the dominion of the group and by ultimately humiliating the leader of the group, men offered an opportunity for the other mature male members of the group to challenge their power and boldness with the male leader, who would be finally injured fatally in his paws or face by the attack of two or three young lions.

Carla was hopeful to witness a disability case and rush for help, though she was far from wishing it to happen. She set up the Radio Telesthesia and examined the pictures that had been taken by the aircraft cameras at the time of landing, and scanned her favorite scenes. By that way she wanted to obtain the characteristics of the leader of the lions and see if any lion of that group had got his classification label.

She stopped at the picture in which the leader of the group was in the center, and scanned it. She put back some frames and zoomed on his head, and scanned it again. Then she opened the comparison program menu. After 1.7 second the computer showed an illusion of the lion just eight meters behind her, in three dimensional live form and sound.

Carla closed her eyes quickly and turned round. She knew well what she would confront, and she prepared herself for that. It took three seconds for her to master up her mind. She opened her eyes slowly. She had hardly opened them wide enough when she was petrified by what she saw.

She was inclined to believe her eyes. She knew that the apparition was just a fantasy, yet she believed what she saw completely. It was as if the logic and calculating parts of her mind had gone void in a moment. She started to breathe again, after her momentary shock. In that brief moment she beheld the very incarnation of power, eminence, and dignity, which she had supposed in her life she had a portion of them. Her experience was so lifelike that the image on the hologram frightened her.

She stretched her hand slowly towards the keyboard and pressed a key. The image faded and dissolved like a veil of smoke, and the wall of her compartment appeared before her, with just 1.5 meters distance.

She had lost her self-confidence in her self-control. Yet it was not what beset her. She was bothered lest she would play an indirect role in that aforementioned 65% damage. She turned toward her computer again. At the time the measured sizes of the male leader of the group had appeared on the monitor. The net weight, excepting a 40 kilos meal of a hunt was 270 kilos, which meant the lion was over 310 kilos when he was full up with food. The length of the manes and neck were equal to 1.2 of the average male heads of African lions. It meant that he was an extraordinary lion, and was even larger than Bengal tigers or the exceptional species of Siberian tigers.

There were just five lions as huge as him, according to recorded cases.

Carla reviewed the recorded files and found that neither the leader of nor any other lions of the group carried classification labels. That big fault, however, seemed very unlikely. With those very advanced satellite and computerized facilities that the National African Parks had been provided by the organization, the data of the lions of that group should have been recorded somewhere in the organization, and at least one of the lions should have been marked by laser canons, but Carla found nothing, despite her persistent searching.

She wasn't annoyed or angry, though, of the lack of those data. She was even happy. That would offer her an exceptional opportunity to work on them, giving her a chance of taking samples or making surgery on them, if it proved necessary.

She glanced at her watch and began preparing for her trip. She took off the standard boots of the organization and put on a pair of light shoes made of clothes which absorbed the least noises of walking. She hung the Radio Telesthesia from her neck and wore the special night glasses. She stole out of her compartment and walked towards the jeep. She thought of carrying the Wilson rifle or the PN 7, but then she changed her mind. "I am not going for hunting or for animal rescuing operation," she told herself, "This air handgun is just enough."

The air handgun she carried was used for anesthetizing animals in zoos from a short distance. She wasn't sure, however, that even two or three of those two-stage bullets would be enough for that leader lion of the group, if she happened to confront him. She set out, however. She passed through the two rays of blue laser light which were designed as an additional barricade for wild animals, and disappeared in the darkness of the meadow.

Chapter 3

Although Steve Blake had broken too many English habits and traditions to be regarded as a typical Englishman, he had still remained faithful to one Englishness, and that was his punctual going to bed. This punctual practice of Steve had not abandoned him, despite peculiarities o of his profession, which demanded irregular urgencies. He was just going to sleep, with that common experience of pre-sleep thoughts giving way to thorough tranquility, when an overwhelming thought harassed his mind, and he was wide awake in a moment. He sat up in bed and thought something bad was happening, he felt somehow, but he didn't know what it was. It was an instinctive feeling. He decided to have a look around and see Carla and the camp.

He got up and went out of his compartment.

Carla was inside the meadow. The grass was sometimes as tall as her shoulders. She advanced for the trees. There was little likelihood of a loin herd being there, for the range of the waves that scared the animals away extended at least 20 meters farther than the last tree, yet Carla expected to be attacked by a lion any moment. A lion might leap on her from behind or from above a tree. She kept her finger on the trigger of her air hand gun, ready to pull it. She was confident of herself, however, as she was able to see the utter darkness of the Sahara Desert, thank to her night eye-glasses, even better than the lions.

She went towards a tree, which was the farthest from the camp, and leaned against it. Then she strode back towards the camp with elaborate big steps, counting her paces and stopping at 20. She was now in at the border of relative security and numerous perils of the wilderness, the zero point between the two. She decided to start her work from that spot.

She lay down on her elbow, with her back to the camp. She cut some of the grass beneath her which were making rustling noises, and made a cushion of them to lean her elbows. She then turned on her Radio Telesthesia and put its helmet on her head. She opened the monitor of the helmet which was as large as her hand, and put it before her eyes. She could then survey her surrounding by the angle of 360 degrees, in a full circle of up to 2 kilometers of diameter.

She could select any animal by the application of a tiny mouse, and focus on any particular one. She turned on the distance-measurer to specify the distance of the nearest animals, if there were any luckily, there was nothing behind or around her, for the moment, and the nearest creature before her was 630 meters away. But after a few seconds she noticed that the distance decreased suddenly and reduced to 505 meters.

Carla tried to conjecture the kind of creature, before using her Radio Telesthesia to specify it. With that speed and power of the brute she reckoned it was a young panther. But what was the reason for that tremendous speed of a lonely panther, if it wasn't after a quarry? It must have chased a deer or something, she thought, but the Radio Telesthesia had just specified a single animal. Carla thought perhaps the instrument had confused the two animals, the hunter and the hunted, due to their closeness together, by the interference of waves, though the fault probability of the device was just 0.0001. She reset the instrument. It took 36 seconds. In the meantime Carla remembered that she was to analyze the scanned images of the leader lion by the Radio Telesthesia and obtain his behavior factors. She regretted that she hadn't done this before, and she wished the beast to be within the 2 kilometers range of her instrument, to provide her with the opportunity to work on him.

Carla's unusual interest for the feline in general and lions in particular was mainly because those beasts did have human passions such as hate, ambition, jealousy, and revenge, and triumphed over those passions and thrived on them, if they met the occasion. This included felines among the most dreadful of animals.

Suddenly Carla remembered that she had the mini-CD containing the scanned images of the beast. She took it out of her pocket and put it in the driver of the Radio Telesthesia. Then she ran the main menu and clicked the relevant keys and waited. She clicked some more keys and then divided the device area into two separate sections, in order not to be wholly unaware of her surrounding. The first section functioned as analyzing images and showing the results, while the second section offered, simultaneously, both the type of behavioral signs and the distance of the animals around.

The time allotted for both the programs was one minute, but as the image analysis program had started earlier, it finished its function first. Six different types of behavioral signs appeared on the monitor, one by one: the first was an utter fright, then a sense of escape from danger, and then disillusionment, anger, and at last, hate and revenge. Another sign was added to the rest, with some delay, and that was smile. But it was incongruent with the rest. Moreover, the distance was also specified at the bottom of the monitor, and it was just 8 meters. But the distance was not significant in this section of the program.

Carla stopped for a moment. She found herself watching the second section of the program. Her wish had been fulfilled and she was analyzing by her Radio Telesthesia, the live behavior of the leader of the lions, who was just 8 meters behind her. He smiled with satisfaction as she triumphed over gaining control of a lion of the group that had been scared and flown away from their dominion that day, by the landing of the aircraft.

She shivered as her huge neglect dawned upon her. She realized her peril. With the least movement of hers she would be torn to pieces. She turned round and lay on her back and smoothly aimed her air hand gun at the lion's forehead. She pulled the trigger four times, shooting all the bullets in the cartridge. The needles of the bullets penetrated deeply into the beast's head, and Carla heard four short wizzing reports of the shots, which were her last hope, yet the lion was gaining at her Carla quickly. She waited for the second stage of the bullets' action, but the brute was still coming to her, though with a little slackened paces now. There was just 3 meters distance between the beast and Carla, when the animal stiffened his muscles, bent a little on his hind paws, and dived at Carla.

The lion was in the air when there was a report of a gun, and he span around himself by the spasm of the shot and nearly collapsed on Carla. Carla rolled quickly aside and dodged in time, before the heavy animal fell on her. The bullet that was shot by Steve had pierced through the animal's body, as it was aimed at a short distance. The wounded lion got up quickly, despite the damage, and vanished in the darkness.

Before this adventure, Steve had got out of his compartment, just in case. He had called Carla's compartment and knocked but had heard no reply. He had tried to contact her through **visiphone**, a sound-visual transmitter and receiver, still with no avail. Then he had gone to the entrance door to the provisional store and checked the laser protection system. The numerator had recorded one instance of an intelligent pass. This was Carla, without doubt, because if any animal had passed through, even if it had dared to ignore the infrasound waves and proceeded, the remains of its body would have been scattered around the laser bars. There was no beast as bold as that, as far as Steve knew.

He rushed towards the jeep, took the Wilson rifle, applied the smell-removing spray on his body, put on the night eye-glasses, passed through the two beams of laser rays, and set out. But his steps were hesitant. He wondered where to go. A quick review of the events of that day gave him an idea, and started towards the trees.....................

Steve tried to walk silently, yet his movement through the grass was conspicuous. He walked for some minutes and then stopped to survey his situation. He wasn't very far from the trees, and with that pair of night eye-glasses he was able to see even the leaves distinctly and vividly, yet he couldn't see Carla through the thickness of the foliage and the bushes.

"Where the hell has she gone?" he asked himself, "She might have passed the security range of the camp by now. I hope she has used the spray. Or else …"

Suddenly he saw a huge shadow coming to him. He stopped breathing and the shadow approached nearer. Steve gripped at his gun firmly, ready to shoot any moment. The shadow kept coming closer and closer, until it passed Steve by, hardly one meter away. Steve could smell the animal. It stalked professionally, as a hideous night predator does, and curved its haunting way towards the trees.

Steve started to breathe, but waited to gain a reasonable distance from the animal. Then he bent the tall grass and peeped after it, and saw the powerful sinewy shoulders. It was a lion, and a very large one. Steve could hardly persuade himself that he had seen the animal within the security zone of the camp.

What could draw the creature into the zone of the infra-sound rays? It wasn't a quarry, of course, because there was no alive being at that area except him and Carla. He struck on the apparent idea at last. Yes! Carla!

Steve followed the animal at a cautious distance, trailing it by the direction of the grass that was trampled by the lion.

The lion came to the trees and climbed up of the biggest one, and looked around, sniffing at the air. Steve was motionless, as an Egyptian mummy. The lion climbed down the tree softly and started towards the opposite direction from the camp, stealthily. As he was ten meters away from the trees, he raised his head and purred. He was likely intending to be seen by somebody.

Steve sensed the danger and approached the lion with the least noise. He took off the night eye-glass and looked through the telescopic sight of his rifle. He first scrutinized the lion and then the surrounding of the animal.

He saw Carla lying on her back on the grass, petrified, and then heard muffled sound of air-gun shots and then ..., and when he saw the expression on Carla's face he knew that he must do something. He turned to lion quickly and aimed his rifle at him. The brute was in the air and there was no time for a between-the-eyes-shooting. He fired, just to save Carla. He was a good marksman, having practiced a lot with that rifle during his training, but the force of explosion was more than he calculated now, due to his nervousness and hurry, and therefore he had his shoulder knocked by the kick, and he almost fell, but he grasped the rifle and ran towards the spot, arming the rifle for a further shots.

The brute had run away, despite his bleeding, which was noticeable on the grass. Carla was lying on her back, still unable to analyze her present condition. Steve reached her, asked if she was all right, and didn't wait for her reply. He felt her limbs to find if she had any serious cracks or injury. Carla was all right, and she said it. She rose slowly and sat up. They both sat on the grass for a while.

Steve was looking for an excuse, to start talking and blaming, when the Radio Telesthesia caught his eye.

"What the devil is this?" he asked, "A Pandora box?! It doesn't look as a tool of our project."

"It is Radio Telesthesia," said Carla.

"A new computer game, eh?" said Steve, "The Most Dangerous Game! The End Game! The ..."

"Not now." interrupted Carla. She was resting her arms on her knees and holding her head with her hands.

"What not now?" pursued Steve.

"Not now, Steve, please!"

"But I need to talk to you, about things we must do and things we mustn't, both. Let me ..."

"You want to clarify something again, yes," interrupted Carla, "But I am not in the mood now. I am aware of what I have done, and why. I am highly grateful that you saved my life, but should I be your tame slave as the reward? Did you want to clarify this?"

Steve felt secretly happy for Carla had called him as he wished, yet he pretended to be angrier than before and said, "As soon as I reach the transmitter, no danger will threaten you." He read the question "How?" in Carla's sad but unquestioning eyes and went on, after a short deliberate pause:

"Let me tell you how. When I give my report of the accident and your willfully adventures, you will be summoned surely, and this time I don't think uncle Hans can do any significant thing. And if you think this project is too important to be cancelled and replaced by other people, I must tell you that you are mistaken. You are too dear to be served as a pre-meal for a hungry uncivilized African lion."

Steve couldn't stop his bitter jokes even in situations like that. Carla wanted to answer him but withdrew. She asked with a normal tone, "Is it over?"

Steve stopped and looked down, sensing that he had been a bit cruel. Carla went on:

"First of all, if it had not been your untrustworthy Englishness, your unnecessary interference, I would have managed somehow. Second, you have taken the matter too seriously, making it hot. Third, why I call you untrustworthy? Because, if you hadn't had such a reaction; which I predicted before. I would have told about it to you. And now, if you don't have anything more to clarify, I am going back to the camp."

She began gathering her things.

By now Steve was really angry. He said, addressing himself:

"You are stupid and 'untrustworthy' Steve! Why didn't you give a chance for Carla to 'manage' with a hungry and a more-stupid-than-you lion?"

He said nothing more and started beside Carla towards the camp. Carla knew that she had been unjust. She waited for a moment to make an apology. They were walking through the grass without words or glances.

Carla strode ahead and then turned and faced Steve. Steve tried to pass her by but she took his hand and stopped him. She looked into his eyes and said, "You did a great job and I appreciate that. Things were said which mustn't be said. But you should admit that you were somehow to blame. That 'uncivilized' 'hungry' African lion was an exceptional case for me. But ..." Steve interrupted her and mocked the rest of her conversation: "But Oh Steve! I thank you for you had your shoulder damaged when you tried to save me." And Carla concluded: "But I thank you." The last word was uttered softly, and was accepted by Steve, who was naturally calm ... person. She went on, "And I am sorry for your shoulder. I'll examine it as soon as we get to the camp." And then she added, just as a joke, "Though it was your own fault, as you had practiced on this rifle before."

"Oh God!" cried Steve, but not seriously, "This is I who has to apologize."

They were both smiling as they came to the blazing laser bars. They entered the store and Carla examined Steve's shoulder. It wasn't seriously damaged. Carla applied an ointment on the swollen bruise and they retired to their compartments and fell fast asleep, as they had had an adventurous night.

Chapter 4

Carla got up early the next morning and stole out of her compartment, and began setting a big breakfast table for two. She also put a pair of candles on the table and lit them. Then she noticed an unusual blazing of the laser bars. She turned round and looked. The number of laser beams had been increased from 4 to 16, and the distance between each of them was hardly more than 30 centimeters. She was locked up inside a real prison, because the door between the cabin and the store was locked from inside the cabin. Steve had done this, without doubt; therefore he must be outside himself. Carla approached the laser bars. Steve was out, enjoying the glorious sunrise of African Sahara.

"Steve Blake!" called Carla.

"Yes?" answered Steve coolly.

"May I ask you what is the meaning of this?" said Carla, trying to control her anger. She pointed to the laser bars with her glance.

"I didn't wish to see my trustworthy colleague gone," Steve said, "When I awake, without a trace or calling, to walk among a pack of lions, hyenas, and I know not whats."

Carla went to the other side, towards the laser controlling device, to enter the password and stop the beams. She entered the 6 letters of the password but it proved invalid. She got nearly mad and said:

"Damn you Steve! I am trying to serve you a big breakfast and give you a surprise, but you are trying to make me mad. If I get you… come here quickly and stop this damned thing, or else…"

"Or else what?" interrupted Steve, "or else there will be no food? As for the surprise, I must confess I was thoroughly surprised last night, surprised enough to kill my appetite. You must work hard, if you wish to get out of there. You have to try 268 million number/letter combinations. Of course, you may hit at the password right away, by the first combination! For example, M-Y-L-I-O-N, or … S-T-U-P-I-D-S-T-E-V-E, or E-N-G-L-I-S-H, or S-U-R-P-R-I-S-E, or…"

"Stop and listen!" cried Carla.

"You stop and listen!" said Steve, showing him angrier than her. "Last night you asked me if there was anything to clarify, and I now tell you that yes, there is. First, nobody will go away without informing the other. Second, we will discuss our sensible wishes after the office hours of the project, and if mutually agreed on something, we might then do any foolish suicidal things. I hope I am quite clear."

This was even more than Carla wished. She would have told Steve, with much elaboration and introductions, what Steve said now. She grew calm and said, "All right, what you say. But come and stop this bar for the moment. If you had not done this, it would have stopped automatically by the time of the end of the office hours."

They both grew calm now. Steve was a bit regretful for what he had done to Carla, at the first work day of the project, but that was necessary. If he didn't do that it was not sure what hazards Carla would do next. She might even break down the infrasound wave transmitter.

"Why don't you try it yourself?" Steve said.

Carla was confused, but soon found out about Steve's childish play with her. She entered the letters of her first name C-A-R-L-A, and then added F, and the laser charge resource was turned off! She wanted to give a retaliating response to Steve, but stopped on second. She needed Steve for some of her requests. Steve was surprised and a little happy that Carla didn't get mad. He sat at the table.

Things looked all right, except for one that that disturbed the harmony of that huge breakfast table. That was an ancient German hunting hat, put at the center of the table, between the two candles, one of those hats that Steve never liked. Carla brought the food tray and asked Steve to take the hat from the table so that she could put the tray on its place.

"Where shall I put it, then?" asked Steve.

"Why, on your head, of course." said Carla.

"What?"

"I said put it on your head."

"You are joking!"

"No, I am not."

"What? Put this hat on my head? Make a fool of myself for your fun, and at meal time?"

"Then I must inform your Excellency that this is our family traditional meal, and when it is served in our royal hunting place all the men must have such a hat on their heads, and up to now this tradition has not been broken. And moreover, you had better been informed that you are the first non-member of our family who is honored as such. Yet you don't have to do it, if you don't want to. But if you wish to have this food you must perform the ritual. But if I am not mistaken, you said you have no appetite."

"Oh, no!" mourned Steve.

"Oh, yes!" concluded Carla, and then she began serving food for herself.

Steve turned her head, hoping for Carla to change her mind. He was still holding the hat in his hand, playfully, but the sound of Carla's fork and knife indicated that she was enjoying the food enormously. Its smell was maddening the starving Steve. In fact, when Carla had put forward the hat-for-food business, Steve's appetite rose. He absorbed his saliva, but when he visualized the food tray, with its rich ravishing smell and sight, he gave in.

Steve put the hat on his head emphatically and turned to table to attack the food. He saw that Carla had not been helping herself with the food but waiting all the time for him to start together. The sound of fork and knife was just to provoke Steve.

Steve noticed that Carla was watching his odd appearance and movements, smiling. She served food for both.

"Wait a minute," asked Steve before eating, "Tell me please, is there any other pre-meal or post-meal condition? African dancing, for example, or wrestling with the son of the biggest African gorilla?"

"No, there is not!" said Carla, unable to hide her smile, and stealing a look now and then at the amusing appearance that Steve had made for himself.

Steve devoured the food for which he had made that interesting appearance for himself. He noticed Carla's constant glances and took off the hat forcefully, made an ancient military salutation to Carla, and then put it on his head again, properly.

After the meal when they were sipping their coffees, Steve began the conversation:

"Tell me, Carla; was this royal feast for my sake? Sure you will ask for something in return. Out upon it! No beating about the bush."

"All right," said Carla, seeing Steve so apt for listening. "After we finish planting those laser chargers around the camp, I want you to me a favor and activate the satellite searching channel."

Steve: "But we agreed to talk after the days' work and do anything that both thought it right. I didn't agree to be ordered by you about things outside the project, and that during the office hours. Suppose I accepted this, but you know that we have no right to use that channel except for the number one and number two priorities."

Carla: "I just know that when the duties of the project were being discussed, the channel password was given to you, and not to me. And if you don't do this I will do it myself, by a way or another.

29

Steve could guess what Carla meant. She might hazard both their lives and the whole project by her reckless exits from the camp. He said:

"In return for this meal you put such a big hat on my head.[1] But beside this, please give me a good reason to convince me that why I should do this risk. If your reason is convincing, I'll be with you."

Carla said, "Then listen: Last night I took the blood sample of the lion that shed on the ground. Also, before the attack I had had a creature on my Radio Telesthesia range that moved 125 meters in 5 seconds, that is, 90 kilometers per hour. At first I thought it was a panther, hunting for a prey, and I thought perhaps an interference of the waves had caused the reception of the signals of just one animal, and this was my mistake. I reset the instrument and during that short period the animal had approached me with an unusual speed for a lion. He had circled my sight range and approached me from behind. His initial speed was probably for deceiving us, in case we had him in view. The prodigious point about it is that it has penetrated inside the security zone of the infrasound waves, 40 or 50 meters, as you said. I think these acts are motivated by just one sense, and that is revenge."

Carla continued, "I analyzed his blood DNA last night and compared it with the extant genetic samples of an apparently extinct generation of lions that were once living only in the Sahara Desert. They were identical! It means that up to now we have at least proved that the generation of that creature has not been extinct, and there is still a chance for them to survive. Probably none

---

1   In Persian language, "to put a hat on somebody's head" means, idiomatically, to deceive somebody.

of the male members of the pack has as pure DNA as this one, regarding his particular behaviors and his enormous size. And probably he has got 3 to 6 cubs from his mates. If he is still alive, and wishes to come back to his pack in such a condition, the other mature males of the pack will try to take their opportunities to kill him and then his cubs. But if we find him, by the searching channel, and save him, in case he is alive, we will have done a very great job, along with our project of course."

Steve asked, "May I know what you will do with the recorded CDs of the searching channels? You are not going to change or destroy them, are you? And I should tell you that I like my job and need it."

Carla said, "Why do you try to appear more foolish than you are?"

Steve: "Oh, I think I must thank you for the compliment."

Carla: "If we can do this we will be just reprimanded slightly, but then we will have a lot of merits. You don't need to talk about your insignificant job!"

Steve: "I think I have been flattered enough today, Carla. We had better start our work."

Carla: "You can't start and go away without giving me a straight answer."

Steve: "I said we'll talk about it."

Carla: "What talk? There is no talk left. You said you want a reason, and I provided you with one."

Steve was too convinced to resist Carla's quest. Carla was aware of that. She asked, with a half pleading look of her eyes, "I ask you for the second and last time. Please, Steve!"

Steve paused for a long time which indicated his consent, and said, "You are the boss, and therefore you are responsible for all things. But keep it in your mind, Carla, that you forced me into this."

They specified the borderlines of the camp, to be demarcated by the laser chargers that they were going to plant, according to their schedule. A small type of the device had already been planted on the entrance of the aircraft and the storehouse.

The chargers functioned as barbed wire, more efficient and reliable. Even a tank couldn't pass through their burning rays. Then they set up their 20 weeks lodging, which was a very well-equipped pre-structured hall. That was the end of their work for that day. They were free to follow their extracurricular tasks then. It had been their first work day under a baking sun, and they drank a lot of water. They were ahead of the time, despite the hard labor.

After the first day work they rested for half an hour, away from the heat of the sun, inside the newly set up main construction. Its air-conditioning and furniture, and the cold drinks of the fridge made it a heaven at the heart of that infernal Sahara.

After recreation Carla set up the satellite communication system and Steve started to set up the main computer of the laboratory and its 60 inch monitor. The computer, the most important instrument of the project, was to be set up in the hall on the fifth day, and it was to be used solely for analyzing genetic data, but Steve set it up quickly inside the aircraft and connected it to the satellite communication device. He wanted to utilize its remarkable power in data analysis for surveying vast areas of African Sahara, to find the lion.

Steve sat at the keyboard desk to activate a particular satellite channel for their special undertaking by entering the password. He turned back to see if Carla watched. She was just behind him, smiling amiably.

"Please, Carla," begged Steve, "observe this one rule, so that I can claim to myself that I have been committed to one rule at least!" The he added, "If you don't obey, I'll have to tie your hands and legs!"

"No Englishman can do this to me," said Carla, with the same amiable smile, "but OK. You should have said it more kindly. I am going to sit in front of you, so that I cannot see the keys you click, and can not know the satellite channel password, which is probably my first name again, plus my family name initial!"

Carla walked three meters away from Steve and sat looking at him, looking mysterious and naughty.

"O my God!" thought Steve, "Is this a bluff, or does she really know it, that the password is again her first name plus F? How could she know? This is certainly a bluff, but a skillful and a dangerous bluff. I can not change the password because of an impenetrable software lock." He then encouraged himself: "Suppose she knows the password. Firstly, I do what she wants me to do, and secondly, we are colleagues, with so much mutual interests, and the fact that from the beginning the password was trusted to me, because of Carla's willfulness and unpredictable behavior, was a mistake of the organization."

Steve comforted himself by such reassuring thoughts and entered the password, and then clicked some additional keys around the keyboard, to mislead Carla, looking at the keyboard and Carla in the meantime. Carla looked quite calm and content, silently mocking men's way of whistling, and apparently paying no attention to Steve.

Steve entered the channel ordering menu and called Carla: "Here you are. You can now find that foolish creature. I hope he has kicked the bucket by now."

Carla rushed towards the keyboard and said, "Thank you Steve. You are marvelous. But don't talk about my lion like this. You can't imagine how I am interested in that rare creature.

"Then you will be interested in anyone or anything that tries to annihilate you." Steve said, and then added casually, "And so you are interested in that animal more than me?!" This was an unwanted overflow of his feeling toward Carla – his newly sprung love to her - , and he hoped for Carla not to find it out, at least at this time.

"Sure, I am." Said Carla, regarding her rapidly improving relation with Steve, she let herself reply Steve like that. From her reply and her hurry with the keyboard Steve found out that she had not found about his feelings to her. He sighed with relief and went on: "So, you preferred your colleague here to be a lion, and me galloping in African plains after my instinctual needs."

"Can't you understand a joke? Steve?" said Carla, "And yourself always joking …"

At that moment Carla concluded her work with the computer and the menu of comparison Program showed the scanned photo of the lion on the corner of the monitor, comparing it with the scanned photos of all African lions that were being provided by satellite, in 0.001 second. The comparison speed was so high that the photos raced like dust and vanished. After a few seconds all the young and old lions and lionesses of African Sahara were compared by the computer program and discarded. None of them proved to be the one Carla wanted.

They stared at the ending message of the order that lingered on the monitor, with amazement.

"This is impossible," said Steve, "How can this big animal vanish like a bubble."

Carla was amazed too. She reviewed the stages of the program in her mind quickly, and an idea occurred to her. A slight point had been missed. She refreshed the order and added another small order to the previous program, and then reactivated the Comparison Program. She had realized that the appearance of the lion might have slightly altered, due to his bleeding, and the lion's present picture might not be identical to his original one because of his terrible wound. Therefore she restricted the range of the program, and gave the new order, and the speed of the program increased rapidly, as the photos had been scanned before, and all the previous photos were discarded. There was, however, one last photo, scanned recently, at the second stage of the program. It was a photo of the lion that Carla wanted, more haggard and weak than before. He was obviously suffering greatly by bleeding, pain, and probably the other beasts' attack.

Carla entered another order to the computer and leaned back to wait. The live image of the animal appeared on the monitor. The wounded starved beast had torn an unlucky African fox apart and was devouring it. He had not probably eaten such a humiliating meal throughout his life. He had always been the first among his pack to tear the common prey of his subjects.

Carla identified the prey by its broken skeleton and a part of its remaining ear. But the lion's condition was worse. The bullet had pierced through his right paw and smashed the bone.

The animal finished eating and started at an unknown direction, with a sorry state. Carla thought about the path he took, and about his probable destination. An unpleasant idea occurred to her. The lion was likely going towards his pack. He was going to have his last fight with those male members who claimed for power in the pack. He wanted to either prove his authority, even in his present pathetic condition, or be killed.

Carla was now sure that ultimately the lion would be the loser. Something had to be done. She began working with the computer again, with more speed. The picture on the monitor moved far and far, until the wounded lion was reduced to a dot in the picture. There were several other dots on the right side of the picture, which indicated a pack of lions; the pack that was the object of the wounded lion.

Carla found the location of the pack by the panoramic picture and the direction of the lion. She quickly estimated the creature's distance from the pack and the position of both in relation with the camp. Then she took the satellite range finder and told Steve to be quick.

"Wait!" Steve said, "I can't … not come!"

Carla was nearly mad at Steve's inopportune joke, but she laughed with Steve and they set out.

Steve drove the jeep, and Carla showed the direction. She checked once more the things they needed for the trip: the rifle, a missile-launcher that carried anesthetizing capsules, the satellite range finder, some first aid things, some very strong steel belts to bind the wounded lion, and a trailer which was hauled by the jeep.

Steve drove slowly, making Carla impatient.

"You may be aware that there is a gas pedal just under your right foot," protested Carla, "And you can press it when you are in a hurry." Carla put her foot on Steve's and pressed. The car jumped and moved fast.

"Are you crazy? What the hell are you doing?" cried Steve, "you'll make the trailer come on us! Are you going to kill both of us for the sake of that animal?" But Carla was not listening.

"Take your foot off, please!" Steve begged, "You crush my shoe!"

Carla relaxed her foot at last, without looking at Steve. Steve found that she had seen her object through her binoculars, watching it all the time, without realizing what she was doing. She turned to Steve and said, "Reduce speed. Here we are." Steve did so, agitated.

They arrived at the battlefield of the lions, just in time. The wounded lion went towards the lionesses and cubs. He turned and surveyed his surrounding. He purred and coughed and then roared so tremendously, despite his bleeding wound and his meager nutrition; that a lot of birds startled among the bushes and flapped out of their perch, and a pack of zebra drinking water from the river ran away. The younger lions went to their mothers, who surrounded them protectively.

The wounded lion swayed his head, to spread more terror among the surrounding animals.

There were five lions around the wounded lion, the leader of the pack. Two of them withdrew after that great roar. Two others were hesitant; with fear and fretfulness printed on their features. The last one, which was the biggest of the five, yet smaller than the wounded lion, was still considering his chance for confrontation. The two hesitant lions were encouraged by the self-confidence of the fifth lion, and joined him. They approached their target from different angles, and the fifth lion, the leader of the rebels, came nearer, face to face.

The wounded lion watched him with a wrathful face. The wrath on his face was extraordinary. This led Carla to an important point, for which she flattered herself. She discovered that the young lion who faced the wounded lion was probably his own son, because the wounded lion hated him more than his other enemies. The young lion's remarkable size was another confirming fact. To make sure, Carla had to obtain the son's behavioral indicators and compare them with those of his father's, that is, the wounded lion's. If their behavioral indicators matched up to 75%, then they were undoubtedly father and son. She groped for her Radio Telesthesia, but she found that the instrument was not brought because of their hurry.

"Damn it! O Damn it!" she cried.

"Excuse me?" said Steve, suspecting that Carla's curse might have addressed to him. He had stopped the car somewhere hidden from the lions and had put his binoculars aside as he wasn't enjoying the lions' drama as much as Carla was. He then realized Carla's self-reproach and turned to watch the fighting scene with unequipped eyes.

Carla handed the satellite range finder to Steve, as she was watching the scene through her binoculars, and said, "Seems you have more free time. Please record the scene and scan all the lions' photos."

"Yes, you're Majesty!" said Steve.

"But I said 'please'!" said Carla.

"All right, you're Majesty!" said Steve.

"And after that is done," went on Carla, "be ready to move. You'll shoot the wounded lion by the missile and I'll try to scatter the other lions away. By the way, I'll tell you something that may make you interested in this adventure: the leader of the rebellious lions is the son of the wounded lion."

"Oh enough!" said Steve, "I'm completely interested now."

"Well, don't believe if you don't want to, but I thought you have realized by now that I am not as joker as you, especially on this particular case."

"If you are right, and he is his son," said Steve, "why aren't you making peace between them? to end the conflict happily, so that they may invite us for the peace-making feast, for a royal zebra steak dinner?!"

Carla shook her head with disappointment.

"OK. I was just joking." Said Steve, "but seriously, how can I aim at that wounded animal, and drive the car at the same time, while you are frightening the others away?"

"It is easy to shoot at him. He is wounded and can't move fast, as you exploded his paw!"

Steve stopped arguing with Carla, knowing that it might lead to some serious conflict. He just nodded his approval.

Carla looked through her binoculars to the battlefield and said, after a while, "Move now, quick!"

At the time Carla and Steve were arguing, the wounded lion dug the earth with his left unwounded paw and raised dust and earth to the air. His son couldn't raise as much dust, and this was an advantage point for the father. He knew that his son was as intelligent as him, and he would make the most of his father's physical deficiency, attacking at his wounded paw. In that case the other two lions would attack and finish him. Therefore, everything depended on the first blow, which he intended to bestow upon his son's face. If it proved to be fatal, then all the rivals would leave the battlefield.

The son skulked to the father slowly until they stood vis-à-vis, and they gnashed at each other. The other two lions kept their cautious distance, waiting for the beginning of the fight, to use their chance to act.

The son gave a heavy blow on his father's face, but the father was experienced enough to receive such blows. He dodged. He didn't react seriously for that charge and just gnashed his teeth. He wanted to provoke his son for further attacks, so that he could give him a fatal blow at an appropriate time.

The son grew angry, as he had been humiliated by the father. He aimed a heavier blow, and the father seized the opportunity. He stood on his injured paw painfully and with his left paw afflicted the most fatal blow on his son's face. Blood flew from the deep furrows that the matchless claws of father had made. However, when the father wanted to withdraw his paw, his claws were entangled in the snarl of his son's thick mane. This time the son seized his opportunity, despite his great pain, and gnawed at his father's paw. The conditions were then reversed. This small incident was going to change the fate of the father who was the winner a few seconds before. The father's sound paw was trapped inside the son's strong jaws. He couldn't keep his balance on his injured paw, and he fell. This was going to be his worst and last event of his life. He knew that those coward rebels would soon attack him from behind. He felt the pain of their fangs sinking into his flanks, and waited for more pains, but an overwhelming apprehension made him forget those pains, as he heard the same terrible sound that he had heard the night before, when he had his paw smashed. The report was repeated severally. All the enemies, rivals, lions and other animals started and escaped, leaving him with a pair of two-legged thin creatures who approached him, perched on a hideous monster. The lion knew the smell of one of them, the one he had attempted to attack the night before. What could he do?

The lion knew, instinctively, that if he ran away, in such a condition, the danger would inevitably follow him from behind, but if he rushed towards the danger, there might be some hope.

He rose and limping charged at the snarling monster that came steadily and without leaping, towards him.

Steve laughed secretly at the wounded animal's foolish attempt to attack and told himself, "Come on! Come closer you fool. You'll make it easy for me." He stopped the car and put an anesthetizing capsule inside the missile launcher. The gun was of a high technology. It didn't use injection method, like the air-gun that Carla had used the night before. The missile containing the capsule was going to explode over the target's head, quite harmlessly, and a dense cloud of the drug was going to wrap the creature and make it unconscious by his inevitable inhalation. The cloud would vanish in a second.

Steve waited for the lion to come closer. He put the creature in the + of the telescopic sight and fired. The wounded lion tried to stand up but the dose of the shrouding drug was too strong for him. He took one more step and collapsed in the middle of it, in spite of himself.

Carla and Steve took the trailer towards the lion. Steve started the small but strong motor of the lift and carried the special metal board beside the lion's body. They rolled the unconscious animal on it and Steve started the motor again, using the reverse gear, and lifted the lion and put it on the trailer.

Carla gave two injections to the wounded flank and paw of the lion, to prevent infection and also premature consciousness. Then they tied him with strong steel belts on the trailer and linked it to the jeep.

Steve drove the car towards the camp.

Chapter 5

As soon as they came to the camp Steve cleaned an area of 9 meters square to put up a field hospital tent and then antisepticised it. Carla began preparatory operation on the animal, such burning the edge of his wounded by laser and taking X-ray photos to specify the place where the bone had to be cut off. She noticed that if the bullet had struck 3 millimeters closer to the main bone nothing could have been done and the paw had had to be cut off up from the elbow.

Steve had finished his work, making the operating room ready. "How is it?" he asked.

"Excellent!" said Carla, "Look at this radiophoto." She held the lion's X-ray photo to the setting sun. "What a wonderful shot! I wonder why you didn't smash his brain by such careful aiming!"

"Don't start, please," said Steve, "I promise I will wait on him next time and watch, until your last bone is chewed, and then I'll shoot at him. I give you my word of honor!"

"All right, if your wisecracks are over, let's go and start our job."

"I suppose they are."

Carla went to her compartment and brought a box which contained her secret instruments. She drew a Titanium paw from it. It had some neural threads, consisting of two very flexible photo fiber threads. She connected them to a special socket of the computer and sat at the keyboard.

She gave some orders and some particular keys were determined to transmit neural messages of the brain.

Steve stared at her box and then at the false paw and asked, "What is this, a magic box? I thought your Radio Telesthesia the most amazing, but now I don't know what to say about this."

He was amazed more when he noticed that the size of the paw was very flexible, capable of matching with that of a very young lion or the biggest, even bigger than the paw of that huge crippled lion.

"O my God!" he exclaimed, "I must expect new things to happen all the time."

Carla clicked a key, sending a neural message, and the blazing claws stuck out with amazing speed.

She sent another message which made those straight claws curved. Their sharpness, Steve was sure, was enough to split a rock into two. They could be straight, like a saw, to cut the flesh and bones of a prey, and curved, to enable the animal to climb a tree with the least energy and time. The design was really genuine. Steve admired Carla in his heart and said:

"I have done a favor to the poor animal then, by smashing his paw. If I hadn't done that, you would have probably done so!"

"Steve, don't talk rot. It was inevitable, according to the statistics that I gathered."

"You know, if I were a lion I would love to give away all my four legs, just for the sake of this one."

Steve's funny comparison made Carla laugh. She said:

"It is enough. We must finish the job. We have a lot of other things to do."

She disconnected the paw from the computer and took it to the operating room. Steve went to the trailer and carried it to the operating room. The surgical operation started.

Carla cut off the wounded paw by laser. Then she separated its neural threads and grafted them to the photo fibers of the false paw by the use of neural cells of a laboratory-made creature. In the joint between the photo fibers and neutral threads she also planted a microchip which would transform the animal's brain messages to electromagnetic signs for the photo fibers. The energy that the microchip consumed would be provided by the natural heat of the animal's body.

The job was almost over.

"What now?" Steve asked.

"What do you mean?" said Carla.

"I mean, you Guardian Angel, shall we let him at large, when we finish with him?"

"No, we are going to wait on him for a few days. He has lost much blood, which must be remedied. Otherwise a fight will finish him."

"I don't think so, with this favor that you did him. Hey! What about these wounds? Won't you fix them?"

"No, these wounds are common in the world of the wild. They'll be healed up by themselves."

"What if he grew restless? Or wished to do his first experiment with the new paw on you and me? And I must say that when he is conscious the infrasound waves will have a great effect on him, especially because the distance is so short."

"Well, we won't let him grow conscious."

"Hey! Wait a minute!" Steve said with dismay, "What about his meals? Perhaps we will chew his food for him in turns and put it in his mouth?!"

"Why do you start your statements in reverse direction?" answered Carla, "It is obvious that he can't eat when he is unconscious. But we will provide him meat and blood serums!"

"Oh, no!" mourned Steve.

Carla had a hard time in persuading Steve to hunt and kill one zebra in four days and smash and grind its flesh, bone, and blood, to make oral serum for the unconscious lion.

Steve hunted his first zebra. According to Carla's estimation he had to kill two more animals, until the lion's physical stamina was restored. That is, they could set the revived lion at large after 12 days.

Days passed slowly and things were done smoothly. It was the fifth day of the camp establishment. Carla and Steve began setting up the main laboratory and then they carried the computer to its main location. On the fifth day, too, they managed to end their work one and a half hour earlier than required, as they did the days before.

That was the day when the last remains of the previous hunting would finish, and Steve had to set out to Sahara for his second Zebra hunt.

An interesting idea occurred to Carla and she told Steve about it, after the end of their work and their 30 minutes break.

Carla said, "Steve, before you go for hunting, I propose to take the lion out of the camp site and study his behavior in his new situation, when he is bound."

Steve read Carla's mind quickly and found that she wished to see the creature's reaction with her Radio Telesthesia and compare it with human criteria. Whatever she meant, it was a postponement to the safari hunting program and then the bloody job of smashing the animal's body to make serum. Therefore Steve quickly accepted the change in the program. He asked Carla what was in her mind.

Carla said: "23 minutes later the lion will gain consciousness, and that will be the time when we must be outside the camp, outdoors, without those infrasound waves."

Steve: "We must hurry, then."

They hurried to connect the trailer to the jeep, fastened the lion on it and set out.

With his remote control Steve turned out the laser bars of the camp gate as they approached the border of the camp and outside.

After they were a good distance away from the range of the waves, Steve disconnected the trailer from the jeep, and they drove back to keep a reasonable distance from the lion.

The lion was strongly fastened by a kind of plastic steel straps and it never occurred to them that the beast can burst himself free.

A few minutes passed and gradually signs of life grew more apparent in the animal. He grew conscious until he was wide awake, and aware of his situation.

First he became restless and stirred. Then he moved violently, in wild jerks, until the trailer was overturned. Carla was watching the animal by the Radio Telesthesia, never thinking of using the anesthetizing missile. She observed, on the animal's face, the behavioral signs of fear, and then desire for escape from bondage and danger, accompanied by some surprise for his new paw.

Suddenly one of the pins that held the straps hit the ground and shot out, making one of the straps loose. The lion shook himself wildly and released his upper part, and suddenly the claws of his new paw were stuck out by an order issued instinctively from his brain. He tore the second strap apart easily, and he was then completely free.

Steve grasped his rifle and made it ready. He was raising it but Carla interfered. "What are you doing?" she protested, and then she put an anesthetizing capsule in the missile launcher and aimed it at the lion. But the lion dashed out of her range and disappeared in the grass field.

Steve sighed with relief, as he supposed he got rid of the animal. He waited for Carla's curse, but Carla was less annoyed than he expected. She said:

"Well, what else we could do? By this break away the lion showed that he had been restored to normal life very quickly, and this is a happy sign."

"It certainly is." approved Steve, secretly wishing not to see the lion again.

"Well, now we can attend our own business. What is your idea?"

"Yes, sir!" exclaimed Steve, overwhelmed by happiness.

He drove the car back to the camp, hoping for Carla to forget all about lions or other animals.

Chapter 6

That very night, however, Steve's hopes turned to disappointment. After supper Carla went into the laboratory to work for an hour before going to bed. Steve was busy checking his applied software and making a list of them, yet he was growing curious of Carla's actions more and more. At last he was too curious and went to the laboratory. He knocked and entered.

Carla had just entered the password of the satellite channel to the computer and was busy giving some orders. Before Steve could complain she said, "OK. You caught me at the crime. But so what? I now know the password and am using it. Why don't you help me? Instead of objections and complaints? Because I have already entered the channel."

Steve was speech-bound. He could just say:

"It seems that trial is finished and the verdict is given. And I can't object. What are you going to do now?"

Carla was happy that Steve consented so easily. She said:

"I want to trail the lion. Not just for now, but for the whole next week, and after I acquired all his behavioral patterns in one week I'll analyze them from the view of the animal psychology. This is an exceptional opportunity that will not be repeated, for me at least. Will you do this favor to me?"

"Is there any favor undone? So why not?"

"Don't be impertinent!" Smiled Carla. "Now listen. I want to have the lion's pictures recorded all the time, and by Beta rays at nights. I wish to know whatever he does and wherever he goes. To trace him is now very easy because of his unusual appearance and a tiny transmitter planted in his false paw."

Steve entered necessary orders to the computer and the trailing started.

The lion's picture appeared on the monitor. He was lying down beside a huge buffalo's carcass, some part of which had been devoured, and enjoying the evening sun. This was somehow unusual. Normally the females of the pack did the hunting job.

Another unusual point was also seen on the corner of the picture. Carla widened the angle of the picture, making it smaller and revealing more things. Despite the fact that a buffalo is usually hunted by four, five, or six lions, and it is very dangerous for the hunters, Carla and Steve noticed 15 buffalo carcasses scattered around, with deep horrible cuts around their throats, necks, or breasts. The pack of the lions was busy eating around two carcasses. There were also the torn bodies of three unfortunate hyenas who had intended to attend the feast.

Moreover, there was the body of a lion in the scene. Carla guessed the lion to be one of the ones who had attacked their leader from behind.

This wasn't a hunting scene but a massacre. The male leader of the pack had now turned into the greatest and most dangerous killer of African Sahara. Although lions normally couldn't catch hyenas that robbed their food, this lion had killed three of them easily, giving a good lesson to the rest.

Steve and Carla were both moved by the scene, and for the first time Carla regretted the surgical operation that she had done on the brute, causing all the slaughter. Yet she consoled herself, saying:

"The law of the jungle: Kill in order not to be killed."

Steve regarded Carla with a criticizing look and said, "It is done. So if you have no other work I am going to bed."

Carla felt the heaviness of Steve's look. She said, "Thank you. I think I should go to bed too."

They both retired to their compartments, though they could use the main construction bedrooms. They had mutually agreed to use the main construction facilities fully when its setting up was completed, on the sixth day.

The sun of the sixth day rose. That day was special for Steve and Carla. It was the end of their laborious time and the day when the camp would be opened and the main program of their mission should start.

They started their work with more enthusiasm. Steve planted the main transmitter of infrasound waves on top of a 5 meters post. He turned off the previous infrasound wave transmitter which had done its job properly, and turned the new main transmitter on.

At the end of the job they tied a strip to the two chargers that constituted the gate of the camp and stayed outside. Then they cut the strip by a pair of large symbolic scissors that Steve had made for the occasion, and formally opened the camp.

Steve jumped in Carla's way and said:

"Please, after you, ladies first… we welcome you to the camp site and the tropical laboratory of the Research Organization and etc."

"Well," Carla said, "Now that our great job is finished, let's go and meet our Mr. Murderer, eh?"

Steve distorted his face into alternative sadness and happiness, saying, "O my God, first comedy, next tragedy. It makes me sick."

They entered the channel and surveyed the path that the lion had passed during the night before and that day. The lion had covered several big curve routes of up to 6 to 8 kilometers long. Then he had come to a big Baobab tree, and had scared away a variety of animals that had tried to possess the tree. After that he had climbed the tree with a tremendous speed and attacked a tiger that was busy eating his prey on a remote branch of the tree, and had dropped it down the tree. The bewildered tiger had run away, despite its serious wounds. Then the lion had climbed down the tree, like a swift cat, without touching the tiger's prey, and had gone on his way.

Carla explained the behavior of the animal to Steve:

"That unlucky leopard should have known that there are stronger and swifter creatures than him in climbing the difficult parts of a tree."

"What about the path that he takes?" Steve asked. "Is it aimless?"

Carla: "In his apparently aimless path he is looking for his son and the other conspirators, to show them his new paw, along with practicing some small pitiful cuts, of course."

Steve: "I say: shall I shoot at his head?"

Carla: "How do you dare?"

Steve: "I don't dare. It was a joke. Now if the second part of the Serial Killer movie is over, let's go for the feast."

Steve had prepared a party on the occasion of the conclusion of the introductory stage of their mission. He had made a dinner of English traditional food. They exchanged presents. Carla's present to Steve was a necklace made of the claws of the lion's cut off paw, and Steve's present to her was an ornamental key-holder made of the cartridge of the bullet that he had fired to the lion.

They retired for the first pleasant sleep in the main construction bedrooms.

Chapter 7

The purpose of the Organization in designing such a mission in which a limited number of individuals took part in planting the whole establishment in difficult situations, was to train individuals for the more ambitious plans of space missions which the Organization was undertaking at that time. There was an intense rivalry among the first class scientists of the European Union countries and their non-European colleagues such as the Persian chief engineer Saeed Saalvar who had a record of seven space voyages, along with some others from China, India, and Malaysia, to be dispatched to such voyages.

The first work day of the main mission was started without any problem. The first thing Carla did was to open the reservoir of liquid nitrogen which was minus 238 degrees centigrade, and to draw out the basic intelligent (DNA)s and make them reach the ordinary laboratory temperature. Then during the next days and weeks she was to cultivate them in the form of cells, and make them capable of receiving primal neural messages. This was the general aim of the mission. Carla had to do these things by her own initiatives, plus Steve's assistance. The first day finished successfully, and all the purposes of the program were met.

The second and third days passed smoothly. After the end of the work they reviewed the lion's behavior. He had grown calmer than before during those three days, yet he was wandering about to find his chance for revenge. He had killed 27 animals within three days, animal such as zebras, deer, buffalos, boars, and there was even a young rhinoceros among the victims, perhaps the first one that had ever been hunted by a lion alone. He had eaten just 6 of his preys. This indicated that the desire for hunting was increasing in him day after day.

At the end of the fourth day, when Carla and Steve sat down by the computer to review the lion's exploits the day before, they noticed the carcasses of three lions on the way of the lion. They were obviously the same male members of the pack that had attacked the crippled lion. The scene wasn't very far from the place of the pack, and the lion had come back to his pack during the day before and had finished his job.

The beasts had large gashes in their bellies and flanks and had died immediately. He had killed his own son with more brutal wounds.

After this adventure he had moved towards the river of death. The river was full and looked beautiful in first glance, but there were numerous eyes on the surface of water waiting for thirsty awkward animals to drag them into water and devour them. There were crocodiles, seven meters long.

The lion advanced the river and began drinking. He lingered so long at this that attracted a crocodile's attention. The crocodile crept nearer smoothly and without the least agitation of the water, and suddenly it leapt at the lion. The lion gave it a blow with his left paw to make a chance for escape, but his paw was trapped in the crocodile's jaws. Before the crocodile could drag the lion into the water or cut his paw, the lion gave it a blow with his false paw that tore the crocodile's thick skin apart. This incident in Africa was even rarer than a lion's hunting a rhinoceros.

The lion then withdrew his paw from the half-dead crocodile's enormous mouth and set out towards an unknown goal on a straight path. Despite his victory over the crocodile, which was the first in Africa, his left paw was seriously damaged.

Steve and Carla had followed the events until that point, when the alarm bell roared. They rushed to the monitor of the closed circuit cameras that had all the laser chargers in view. The lion had entered once more inside the range of infrasound waves and had advanced 20 meters and stood before the laser bars. Despite the blazing light of the chargers the animal had smashed one of the chargers by incessant blows of his paw and was going to do this for the second charger.

Carla found out the lion's very cunning human-like plan in which he undertook an unexpected daring action by appreciating the absolute power that his new paw had bestowed on him. His fight with the crocodile had been deliberately planned to have his natural paw wounded, so that he could obtain his second false but very efficient paw!

Carla said so to Steve, with a bitter smile. Steve listened thoughtfully and then a heavy silence followed. They were both thinking of the consequences. At last Steve broke the silence:

"We must do something" and then added with a friendly tone, to console Carla: "Dear Carla, I am aware of your feeling toward the animals, especially this one. I understand you, or at least I try to, but now you know well that we have no choice but killing the brute. Considering the present situation …"

Steve's lecture was interrupted by another alarm bell which was louder than the previous one. The lion had finished with the second charger, smashing it to pieces. The circuit was no longer functioning as the two chargers were out of the central security system circuit. Therefore the laser beams around the camp were ablaze for a moment and then went out completely, like a candle when it is finished.

Steve was now more determined to kill the lion. He said:

"I must certainly finish him now. The infrasound wave transmitter was never a hindrance for him from the start. If we sit here doing nothing he will tear the hall door like a tin opener and turn us into ground meat."

He took the rifle and went out of the main laboratory hall.

"For God's sake don't stand as a statue!" he cried to Carla at the door, "Do something! This way I think I am committing a crime. Is this lion for you more important than our lives, and the mission? Please do something!"

Steve rushed out and Carla decided to do something. She took the Radio Telesthesia to observe and analyze the last behavior of the lion alive, to record his last behavioral sign. Carla could guess that Steve was happy now that he had found the opportunity to correct his first mistake of poor aiming, and this time he intended to aim at the lion's head, exactly between two eyes, to finish him properly.

Carla turned on the Radio Telesthesia and put the helmet-like device on her head. She was the lion who gained speed by seeing Steve. His steps turned into leaps. The brute, who was more ambitious than any four-legged species and wanted those two-legged creatures to do with his left paw what they had done with his right one, was going to have neither ambition nor life, after a few seconds. He was going to leave the world of life by a bullet shot by Steve; a bullet that was going to make a fatal fault in his organism.

Carla was intensely sad for a second, and pitied the animal. The lion's behavioral sign at the last moment his life was attained by the Radio Telesthesia, and Carla remembered that she had noticed that behavior in her first encounter with him. That was, a smile, then …, and another smile.